This Walker book belongs to:

_____

_____

For Stephen

First published 1991 by Walker Books Ltd
87 Vauxhall Walk, London SE11 5HJ

This edition published 2008

2 4 6 8 10 9 7 5 3 1

© 1991 Nick Sharratt

The moral rights of the author-illustrator have been asserted.

This book has been typeset in WB Sharratt.

Printed in China

British Library Cataloguing in Publication Data:
a catalogue record for this book is available from the British Library.

ISBN 978-1-4063-1681-0

www.walkerbooks.co.uk

Look What I've Found

Nick Sharratt

WALKER BOOKS
AND SUBSIDIARIES
LONDON · BOSTON · SYDNEY · AUCKLAND

At the seaside Daddy and I went exploring.

I ran ahead

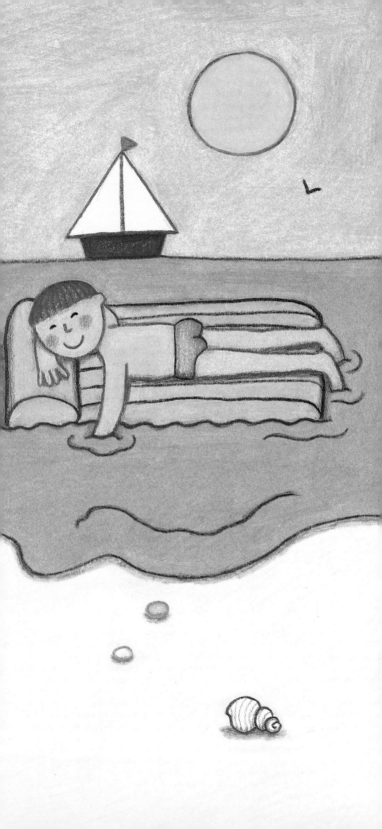

and look what
I found!

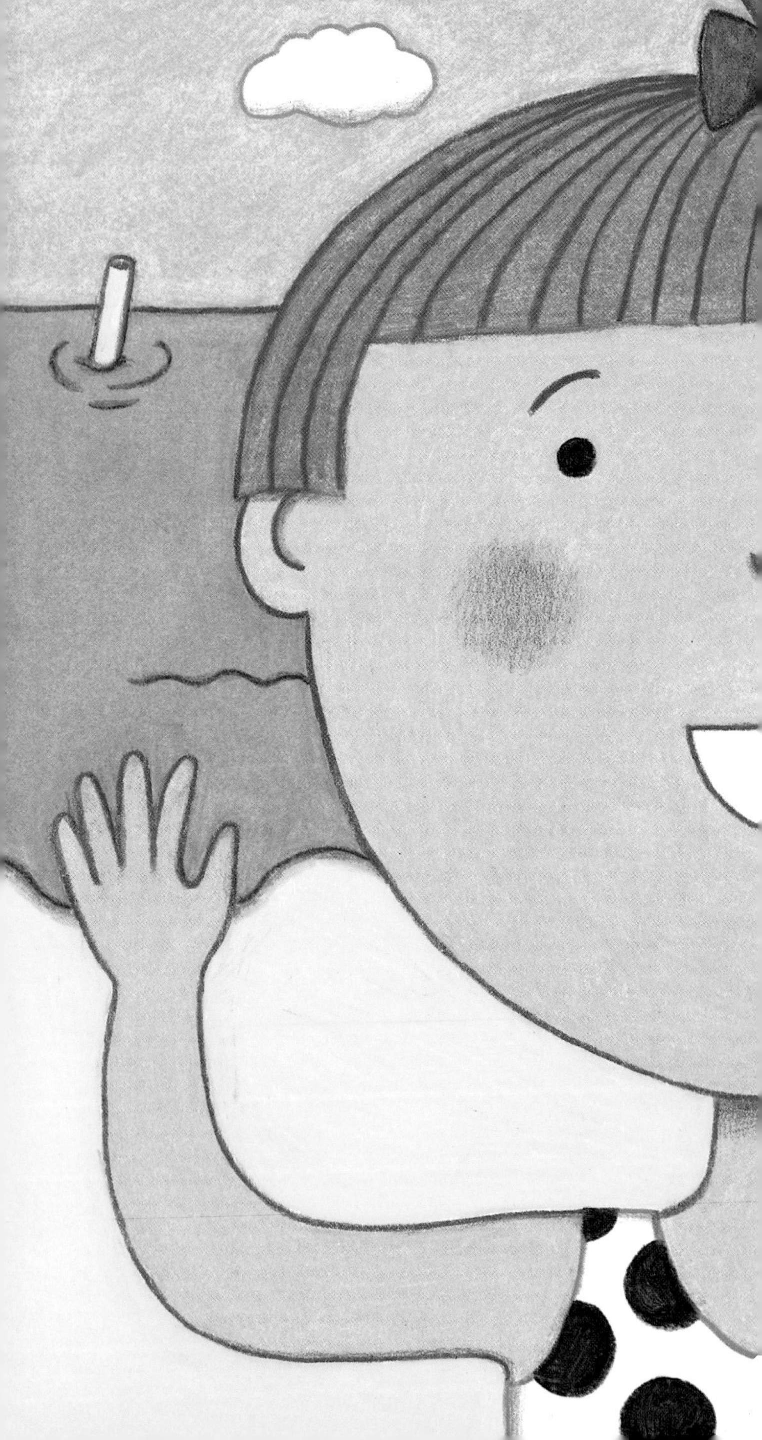

I paddled in the sea

and look what
I found!

I went on the rocks

and look what I found!

I did a cartwheel

and look what I found!

I heard lots of noise

I watched the puppet show

and look what Daddy found!

WALKER BOOKS is the world's leading

independent publisher of children's books.

Working with the best authors and illustrators

we create books for all ages, from babies

to teenagers – books your child will

grow up with and always remember. So…

FOR THE BEST CHILDREN'S BOOKS,
LOOK FOR THE BEAR